—————— Mel Bay Presen

•Tuning the Guitar by Ear•

A practical new approach for the uncompromising musician

by Gerald Klickstein

1 2 3 4 5 6 7 8 9 0

EXCLUSIVE WORLDWIDE SALES AGENT: MEL BAY PUBLICATIONS, INC., PACIFIC, MO.

Visit us on the Web at http://www.melbay.com — E-mail us at email@melbay.com

Contents

Introduction

All guitarists must learn how to tune. From beginners to professionals, guitarists everywhere have to tune before playing. The goal is always the same—to tune as quickly and accurately as possible in order to get on with the real business of playing guitar: making music. The quality of our music-making is built upon the quality of our tuning. Our playing sounds best only when our guitars are in tune.

Over more than a decade, I developed this booklet to serve as a manual for learning the tuning skills that every guitarist needs. It presents an original tuning system that I refined through years of teaching trials. I created it because of a need for improvement in conventional tuning practices and instructions. Of the hundreds of guitarists whom I've taught and observed, few could tune securely using conventional methods. Most guitar students have difficulty tuning and therefore frequently play out of tune. This prevalent lack of tuning skill has two fundamental causes: 1) conventional tuning methods are difficult to use accurately; 2) few materials have been available for *learning* how to tune.

This booklet offers an effective new tuning system and the materials to learn it efficiently. After patiently learning this system, guitarists tune easily and with consistent accuracy. This system is designed in accordance with three accurate tuning principles:

Accurate Tuning Principles

- *Listen for beats* (p. 15). The easiest, most accurate way to tune is by listening for beats (that's how pianos are tuned). Therefore, this system centers on developing the ability to easily hear beats and adjust beat rates.

- *Avoid compounding errors.* In standard tuning, all strings are tested against a single reference string.

- *Learn one step at a time.* Tuning is best learned through an organized approach that builds good *habits*. Therefore, this booklet begins with preparatory information and exercises, then proceeds with string-by-string tuning instructions.

Acquiring fluent tuning skills requires careful study. However, with a moderate amount of practice, any serious guitarist of at least modest ability can learn this system and tune with confidence. Though this booklet is written from my perspective as a classic guitarist, it's designed for *all* guitarists who feel the artistic responsibility to play in tune: this tuning system is equally effective for *all* types of guitars.

How to Use this Book

- *Evaluate your guitar's playing condition and setup* according to the guidelines under *Guitar Fitness* (pp. 5-7). Do this *first*.

- *Begin Getting Started* (p. 9).

- *Proceed one page at a time.* After completing the *Tuning Summary* (pp. 36-37), study the remaining material as needed.

- *Refer to Why this Tuning System Works* (p. 57) and *Questions and Answers* (p. 58) for explanatory information.

- *Refer to the Appendix* (p. 61), for a tuning approach suitable for beginning guitarists.

Acknowledgments

In preparing this book, I'm deeply grateful for the irreplaceable assistance of Dr. Alan Hirsh, who created the computer graphics, edited much of the text, and gave steadfast counsel. Over more than three years, Dr. Hirsh unselfishly worked to aid my development of the fundamental design of this book. I'm also grateful to the many other friends and colleagues who contributed to the creation of this work: Eminent guitar pedagogue Dr. Aaron Shearer made important editorial contributions. Dr. Stanley Yates and Mr. David Leisner assisted with the book's organization and made valued editorial suggestions. Guitarist and piano technician Mr. Roger Peirce gave expert advice, as did Mr. Bill Huesman—master piano technician at the North Carolina School of the Arts. Mr. John Parris spent many hours evaluating the text, graphics and layout, providing insightful comments and suggestions. Screenwriter Mr. Stephen Fischer offered guidance with the writing. Artist Ms. Michelle Parris helped with layout. Leading guitar maker Mr. John Gilbert evaluated the guitar fitness guidelines. Dr. Robert Yekovich, Dean of the School of Music at the North Carolina School of the Arts, was an unwavering source of support and encouragement. Mr. William Bay, President of Mel Bay Publications, was an enthusiastic supporter of this project and championed this book's publication. Finally, I'm thankful to the North Carolina School of the Arts Foundation, which funded the creation of three prototypes of this booklet.

Symbols and Terms

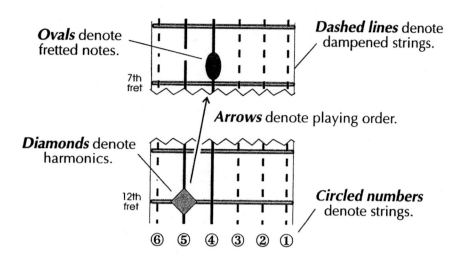

Ovals denote fretted notes.

Dashed lines denote dampened strings.

7th fret

Arrows denote playing order.

Diamonds denote harmonics.

12th fret

Circled numbers denote strings.

⑥ ⑤ ④ ③ ② ①

Fingers are indicated by their international symbols:

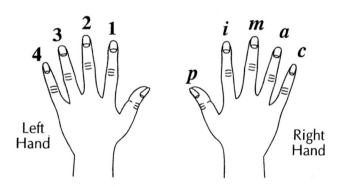

4   3   2   1

Left Hand

i   *m*   *a*   *c*

p

Right Hand

Rest stroke: Play a string so that upon completion of the stroke, the right-hand finger or thumb *rests* against the adjacent string.

Free stroke: Play a string so that the finger or thumb passes freely over and doesn't contact the adjacent string.

Guitar Fitness

For a guitar to be tuned easily and accurately, it must be maintained in good playing condition. A guitar in poor condition will be difficult or impossible to tune. Before learning this tuning system, follow the guidelines below to make a basic evaluation of your guitar's playing condition and to perform simple maintenance. Any additional evaluations or repairs should be done by qualified individuals exclusively.

Strings

Before learning to tune, be sure your strings are in new condition. Replace them if they're not. Old strings produce an impure tone which makes tuning difficult. It's essential that strings be replaced properly. Consult a technician or teacher if you're unsure which strings to use or *exactly* how to replace them. Always replace strings according to the following general guidelines:

Guidelines for Replacing Strings

- *Use high-quality strings.* Low-quality strings often play out of tune.

- *Replace one string at a time* in order to maintain stable tension on the guitar. Avoid removing all strings except for cleaning, adjustments or repairs. Tune each string up to pitch immediately. Tune often to keep the strings at pitch.

- *Pull as much string as possible through the hole in the roller.* First fasten a string at the bridge. Next, fasten the string to the roller in the manner suited to your type of guitar. Classic guitarists should loop the string underneath itself once or twice so that the string overlaps itself when wound around the roller. *Seek assistance* if you aren't certain how to fasten strings at the bridge or roller.

- *Wind each string using the fewest possible revolutions* and cut off the excess string. Neatly winding the least amount of string gives you maximum control when tuning. Excess string wound on a roller reduces a string's stability, making tuning more difficult. Classic guitarists should wind every string so that with each revolution around the roller, the string moves toward the *outside* of the guitar head.

After replacing strings, play the Setup Test (p. 7) to verify that each new string plays in tune and isn't defective. Play the Setup Test periodically to make certain that the strings continue to play in tune as they wear. For maximum longevity, keep the strings clean and play with minimum left-hand pressure. Both dirt and excess left-hand pressure damage strings. This reduces tone quality, affects intonation, and can make accurate tuning difficult or even impossible. Always play with clean hands. If necessary, wipe the strings with a clean cloth after playing.

Tuning gears

The gears must allow precise tuning adjustments. You should be able to lower and raise each string evenly, without skips or loss of control. If you experience problems with any tuning gears, have them checked by a technician. Defective or poor-quality gears are common on inexpensive guitars. They can make accurate tuning very difficult. For ease in tuning, the gears must be of at least average quality and must be maintained in good condition. Keep all screws snug, but not overly tight. The exposed gears on classic guitars require periodic lubrication. Petroleum jelly is a highly-effective lubricant. As needed, *sparingly* apply lubricant to the gear and worm.

Head nut

The strings should move through the grooves easily to permit smooth tuning adjustments. Head nut defects are common on inexpensive guitars. Such defects cause sudden jumps in pitch and loss of control while tuning. You may also hear "popping" sounds. If this occurs, it's often helpful to lubricate the grooves by rubbing them with a little graphite from a pencil point. Do this each time strings are replaced. If problems persist, have the guitar checked by a technician.

Saddle (bridge nut)

The typical classic guitar saddle should be made of bone. It should fit snugly into the bridge groove and have a smooth, curved surface on which the strings can rest without being cut. Discrete notches on the saddle under the strings are usually needed to seat the strings firmly in place. Again, only qualified individuals should make adjustments.

Frets

Each fret should be firmly and evenly seated into the fingerboard. The surfaces should be smooth, with no excessive wear. If any fret surfaces are worn or you hear buzzing on select notes, have the guitar and the frets inspected by a technician.

Action

The term *action* generally refers to the height of the strings above the frets. A correct action makes it possible to play with minimum left-hand pressure. Correct action also allows a guitar to be played loudly without buzzing and to be played accurately in tune. If your guitar is difficult to play or frequently buzzes when played, have it checked by an experienced technician.

Humidity

Extremes of relative humidity can damage a guitar. Maintain a stable humidity level by using a guitar humidifier during dry seasons and by storing your guitar in its case. Guitars exposed to dry conditions or severe changes in humidity are best kept in cases made of synthetic materials which don't absorb moisture. If you use a wooden case, humidify both the guitar and case under dry conditions. Consider purchasing a hygrometer to keep track of humidity levels.

Guitar Setup

For a guitar to be tuned precisely, it must be properly set up. This means that it's accurately adjusted and the strings are in new condition. Before learning to tune, replace your strings (p. 5) if they're not in new condition. Then play the following test to determine whether your guitar is properly set up. *Carefully read all the instructions before playing.*

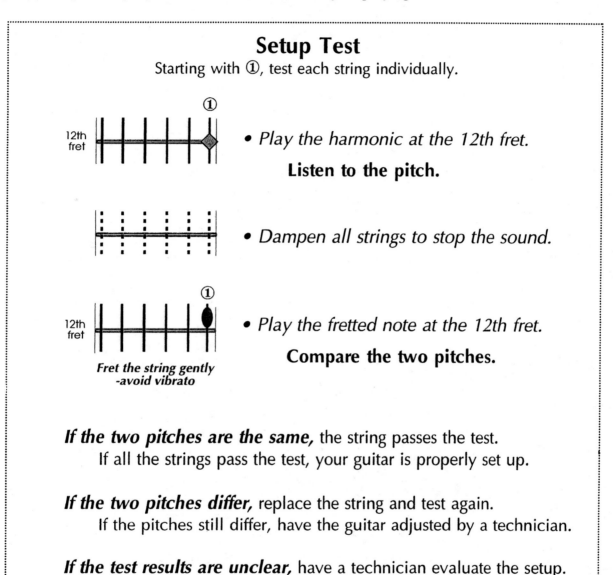

Setup Test
Starting with ①, test each string individually.

①

12th fret

• *Play the harmonic at the 12th fret.*
  Listen to the pitch.

• *Dampen all strings to stop the sound.*

①

12th fret

Fret the string gently -avoid vibrato

• *Play the fretted note at the 12th fret.*
  Compare the two pitches.

If the two pitches are the same, the string passes the test.
  If all the strings pass the test, your guitar is properly set up.

If the two pitches differ, replace the string and test again.
  If the pitches still differ, have the guitar adjusted by a technician.

If the test results are unclear, have a technician evaluate the setup.

Perform this test carefully and repeat it periodically. An improperly-set-up guitar will play out of tune, making any tuning system ineffective. Occasionally, guitars have setup defects which can't be revealed by this test. If you're uncertain whether your guitar plays in tune, have it checked by a technician. *Begin learning this tuning system only after your guitar is properly set up.*

Getting Started

This preparatory section develops the fundamental aural and technical skills needed for fluent tuning. Rapid, accurate tuning is easy once you develop certain refined skills and habits. These include *playing* clearly, *listening* astutely, and *adjusting* strings precisely. Pages 10-13 focus on playing. Pages 15-20 emphasize listening and adjusting.

Always play with the right-hand fingers (not a pick) when tuning by ear. This greatly simplifies tuning. It enables you to dampen unplayed strings as shown in the instructions, thereby preventing sympathetic vibrations. To learn securely, it's best to set aside a little time each day to *practice* tuning. With a moderate amount of careful practice, you'll soon enjoy the rewards of playing exactly in tune.

To learn this tuning system, you need:

- A properly-set-up guitar, in good playing condition (pp. 5-7).

- A good-quality electronic metronome with an A-440.

- The desire for excellence.

Before going further, be sure your strings are in new condition. Old, worn strings produce an impure tone, making accurate tuning difficult or even impossible. *Replace your strings now* (p. 5) *if they are not in new condition.*

Playing Harmonics

When tuning, you'll play the harmonics shown on pages 10-13. Tuning easily involves playing these harmonics *loudly* according to the following guidelines. Practice these harmonics before going further. *Carefully read the instructions before playing.*

12-fret Harmonics

The following 12th-fret harmonics are used in tuning.
Beginning with ⑥, slowly play each harmonic three times.
Listen for *volume* and *sustain*.

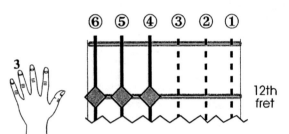

Play each harmonic 3 times.

Left Hand

- Use the 3rd-finger *pad,* not the tip.
- Lightly touch each string over the fret.
- Lift slightly off the string after playing.

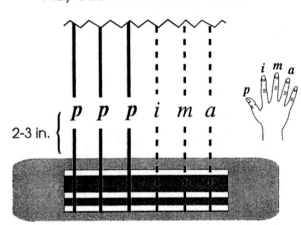

Right Hand

- Place *i, m, a* on ③, ②, ①.
  (to dampen the strings and steady your hand)
- Play forcefully with *p,*
  2-3 inches from the bridge.

7th-fret Harmonics

The following 7th-fret harmonics are used in tuning.
Beginning with ⑥, slowly play each harmonic three times.
Listen for *maximum volume and sustain.*

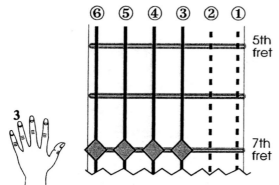

Play each harmonic 3 times.

Left Hand

- Use the 3rd-finger pad.
- Touch *precisely* over the fret.
- Lift after playing.

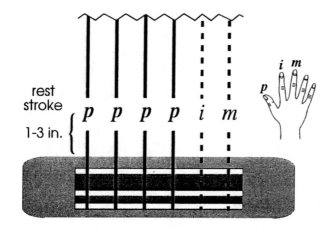

rest stroke

1-3 in.

p p p p i m

Right Hand

- Place *i & m* on ② & ①.
- Play forcefully rest stroke* with *p,*
  1-3 inches from the bridge.
  (Lean your hand toward
   the little finger)

**Rest stroke:* Upon completion
   of the stroke, *p* rests against
   the adjacent string.

5th-fret Harmonics

The following 5th-fret harmonics are used in tuning.
Beginning with ⑥, slowly play each harmonic three times.
Listen for *maximum volume and sustain.*

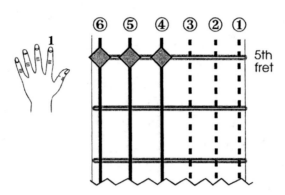

Left Hand

- Use the 1st-finger pad.
- Touch *precisely* over the fret.
- Lift after playing.

Play each harmonic 3 times.

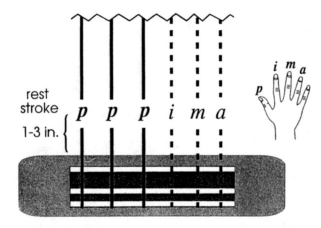

Right Hand

- Place *i, m, a* on ③, ②, ①.
- Play forcefully rest stroke with *p,*
  1-3 inches from the bridge.
  (Lean your hand toward
  the little finger)

Playing Harmonics when Tuning

When tuning, you'll sound two pitches and dampen the unplayed strings. Damping prevents sympathetic vibrations. This produces the clearest sound, enabling you to tune with utmost ease and accuracy. The following two examples are taken from the tuning instructions. Repeat each example several times. Play forcefully rest stroke with *p,* near the bridge. Listen for maximum volume and sustain.

Example 1

Place i, m, a on ③, ②, ①.

- *Play the 5th-fret harmonic of* ⑤.

- *Play the 7th-fret harmonic of* ④.

- *Dampen* ⑥ *with p.*

Sustain both pitches

Example 2

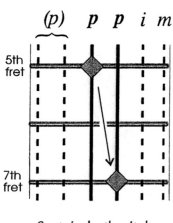

Place i & m on ② & ①.

- *Play the 5th-fret harmonic of* ④.

- *Play the 7th-fret harmonic of* ③.

- *Dampen* ⑥ & ⑤ *with p.*
  (Place *p between* ⑥ & ⑤ to dampen both strings)

Sustain both pitches

Listening for Beats

To tune with this system, you'll listen for sounds called *beats*. Beats are wavering, vibrato-like sounds: *"wah-ooh-wah-ooh."* They occur when pitches sounding together are slightly out of tune. The accurate hearing of beats is a fundamental skill required to tune fluently by ear.

On the following pages are five exercises. They cover the essentials of listening for beats and cultivate habits needed for fluent tuning. Practice these exercises before proceeding further. Subsequent tuning instructions are built upon the foundation established here.

Essential Tuning Habits

Listen! As you practice tuning, you'll become increasingly sensitive to subtle differences in sound.

Play loud, sustaining harmonics according to the guidelines on pages 10-13.

Dampen unplayed strings. This prevents sympathetic vibrations that would make accurate tuning difficult. Throughout the instructions, precise right-hand fingerings are given for both playing *and* damping strings.

Turn the tuning knobs with precision. Turn the knobs with the left hand, *never* the right. Always turn them evenly and decisively. It's also vital that the tuning gears be in good condition (p. 6). Defective or poor-quality gears can make accurate tuning difficult or even impossible.

Before beginning the exercises, tune your guitar to the best of your ability using either an electronic tuner or any tuning system you already know.

Exercise 1

In this exercise you play harmonics on ⑤ and ④ to create a **unison** (two tones of the same pitch). While both harmonics sustain you lower and raise ④, listening for beats as the unison goes in and out of tune. *Carefully read all the instructions before playing.*

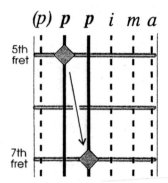

Place i, m, a on ③, ②, ①.

- *Play the 5th-fret harmonic of ⑤.*
- *Play the 7th-fret harmonic of ④.*
- *Dampen ⑥ with p.*

Lower ④ smoothly and stop when beating is clearly heard.
(Lower only enough to hear beats—avoid excessive lowering)

Raise ④ smoothly to where beating stops.
(If you have trouble, start over)

Patiently repeat this exercise several times. Re-play the harmonics as soon as they fade and beats become inaudible. Once you can do it easily, proceed to Exercise 2.

Tuning Tips

Play loud, clear harmonics (pp. 11-13). Play forcefully rest stroke with *p*, near the bridge. Dampen all the unplayed strings as shown.

Grasp the tuning knob promptly. The sooner you grasp, the more time there is to tune before the unison fades.

Turn the knob evenly and decisively.

Exercise 2

Here you play the same unison as in Exercise 1, then *raise* ④ to create the beats.

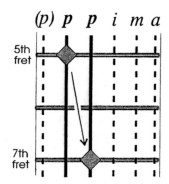

Place i, m, a on ③, ②, ①.

- *Play the 5th-fret harmonic of ⑤.*
- *Play the 7th-fret harmonic of ④.*
- *Dampen ⑥ with p.*

Raise ④ smoothly and stop when beating is clearly heard.

Lower ④ smoothly to where beating stops.

(If you have trouble, start over)

Patiently repeat this exercise several times. Re-play the harmonics as soon as they fade and beats become inaudible. Once you can do it easily, proceed to Exercises 3, 4 and 5.

Beat Rates

In Exercises 1 and 2, notice how the beat rate changes as the unison goes in and out of tune:

The *faster* it beats, the more ***out of tune*** the unison.
The *slower* it beats, the more ***in tune*** the unison.
When ***beatless,*** the unison is ***exactly in tune.***

Exercise 3

To tune each string, you'll play a unison then adjust it to beat at an approximate rate. In this exercise, you learn to *feel* a beat rate—much like you feel a tempo. Only four different rates are used in the tuning instructions. You'll follow this same procedure to learn each one.

Learning a Beat Rate

- *Set your metronome to 88.*

- *Vocalize the sound of beats using the syllables 'wah' and 'ooh.'*

- *Direct the beat rate with your arm as you vocalize.*

Vocalize & Direct:	*wah*	*ooh*	*wah*	*ooh*	*wah*	*ooh*	
MM=88:	tick	tick	tick	tick	tick	tick	etc.

Memorizing a Beat Rate

After completing the above, vocalize and direct the same beat rate *without* the metronome. Aim to establish a comfortable feel for the MM=88 rate. Remember it as precisely as you can without being overly strict. Next, proceed immediately to Exercises 4 and 5 where you'll tune a unison to this same approximate beat rate.

Exercise 4

Here you follow the same two-step procedure as in Exercise 1, then add a 3rd step where you slightly sharpen ④ above beatless. Your aim is to tune ④ to beat gently, at approximately MM=88. *Carefully read all the instructions before playing.*

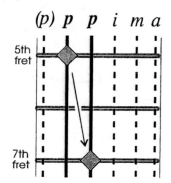

Place i, m, a on ③, ②, ①.

- *Play the 5th-fret harmonic of ⑤.*
- *Play the 7th-fret harmonic of ④.*
- *Dampen ⑥ with p.*

Step 1: Lower ④ so that beating is clearly heard.

Step 2: Raise ④ to where beating stops.

Step 3: Slightly sharpen ④ to beat at approximately MM=88.

Once you complete Step 3:
Play the harmonics then move your left arm along with the beat rate. Compare this rate to MM=88.

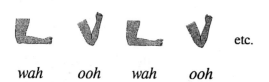

etc.

wah   ooh   wah   ooh

Patiently repeat this exercise several times. Once you can do it easily, proceed immediately to Exercise 5.

Tuning Tips

Develop a feel for the beat rate. Sharpen ④ in the vicinity of MM=88, without being too exacting. If you have trouble, go back to Step 1.

Turn the tuning knob fluently. Lower ④ only enough to hear beats. Raise ④ to beatless with a decisive turn. Sharpen ④ with a keen, subtle movement.

Exercise 5

Here you *flatten* ④ to beat at approximately MM=88.

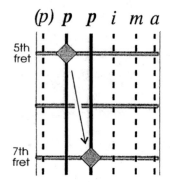

Place i, m, a on ③, ②, ①.

- *Play the 5th-fret harmonic of ⑤.*
- *Play the 7th-fret harmonic of ④.*
- *Dampen ⑥ with p.*

Step 1: Lower ④ so that beating is clearly heard.

Step 2: Raise ④ just <u>below</u> beatless to beat at approx. MM=88.

Once you complete Step 2:
Play the harmonics then move your left arm along with the beat rate. Compare this rate to MM=88.

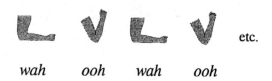

etc.

wah   ooh   wah   ooh

Patiently repeat this exercise several times. Once fluent, you're ready to begin tuning.

Tuning Tip

Always raise a string into tune. This removes slack from the tuning gear and helps a string *stay* in tune.

Learning to Tune

The preceding sections lay the foundation for learning to tune. If you haven't yet worked through this material, do so now before proceeding. As a review, answer the following five questions. If all five answers are "yes," you're ready to begin tuning.

- Are your strings in new condition?

- Is your guitar fit and properly set up? (pp. 5-7)

- Can you play loud, clear harmonics? (pp. 10-13)

- Do you own an electronic metronome with an A-440?

- Have you successfully completed Exercises 1-5? (pp. 16-20)

This tuning system follows a simple design. You tune a string, then test it to ensure accuracy. After tuning and testing all the strings, you play test chords. If the chords sound good, your guitar is in tune. Once skilled, you'll need only one to two minutes to accurately tune your guitar.

The instructions are designed for learning to tune one string at a time. Practice each string's procedures by repeating them until you're fluent. It's best to adopt a comfortable pace that allows you to absorb the procedures easily. For less experienced students, an often appropriate learning pace is one or two strings per week. For more experienced guitarists, one or two strings per day. Advanced guitarists can occasionally learn the entire system in only one sitting. Whatever the pace, after learning to tune all six strings, use the *Tuning Summary* (pp. 36-37) to practice and memorize the system.

To learn quickly, it's vital that you tune correctly from the start. Therefore, *always read the instructions before playing.* Pay close attention to the string damping. It poses a small challenge at first, but makes it possible to tune with utmost ease and accuracy.

Tuning the Fifth String

The fifth string is tuned to the A-440 from your electronic metronome.* This is the standard pitch used by all musicians to tune their instruments. Once tuned, ⑤ provides a reference for tuning the remaining strings. *Carefully read the instructions before playing.*

Tuning ⑤

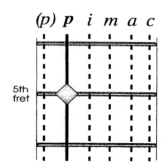

A-440

5th fret

Place *i, m, a, c* on ④, ③, ②, ①.

- *Sound the A-440.*
- *Play the 5th-fret harmonic of* ⑤.
- *Dampen* ⑥ *with p.*

Step 1: Lower ⑤ below A-440 so that beating is clearly heard.

Step 2: Raise ⑤ to where beating stops: ⑤ is now in tune.

Practice tuning ⑤ by repeating this procedure many times.
Go back to Step 1 if you have trouble.

Tuning Tips

Play a loud, clear harmonic (p. 12). Left hand: touch precisely over the fret with the 1st-finger pad. Right hand: play rest stroke with *p*, near the bridge. Dampen all the unplayed strings as shown.

Turn the tuning knob fluently. Lower ⑤ only enough to hear beats. Avoid excessive lowering. Raise ⑤ with an even, decisive turn.

Match A-440 as best you can. If you have difficulty hearing beats against the metronome, match the pitches as closely as possible. As your tuning skills improve, you'll hear beats more easily. Be sure to use a good-quality metronome with a fresh battery.

---

*The metronome has proven the most convenient source for A-440. A tuning fork can be used instead, but students often find it awkward to handle.

Tuning and Testing the Remaining Strings

After the fifth string is tuned to A-440, each of the remaining strings is tuned using a two-part process: 1) *tuning*—where pitch is adjusted; 2) *testing*—where tuning is evaluated. This combination of tuning and testing makes it possible to tune with utmost accuracy and confidence.

Each string is *tuned* using a procedure like either Exercise 4 or Exercise 5 (pp. 19-20). You sound a unison, lower the string being tuned, then raise it to an approximate beat rate. Some strings are sharpened as in Exercise 4. Other strings are flatted as in Exercise 5. To play each unison, you sound two harmonics or a harmonic and an open string. No fretted pitches are used. In this way, your left hand is free to turn the tuning knob while the unison sustains.

After raising a string into tune, you immediately check the tuning by *testing* with a unison involving a fretted pitch. If a string's tuning unison is adjusted to the correct beat rate, then the testing unison is beatless. To prevent compounding any errors, all strings are tested against the fifth string.*

Essential Tuning Habits

Read the instructions before playing. Get it right the first time.

Tune patiently. Fluent tuning skills evolve from careful practice.

Listen! Let your ear guide you.

Tune from below. Always *raise* a string into tune. This removes slack from the tuning gear and helps a string *stay* in tune.

Practice! Repeat each new procedure many times.

---

*See: *Why this Tuning System Works* (p. 57) and *Questions and Answers* (p. 58) for a more detailed explanation of tuning and testing.

Tuning and Testing the Fourth String

The fourth string is tuned using the three-step procedure from Exercise 4 (p. 19). You play harmonics on ⑤ & ④, then sharpen ④ to beat gently, at approximately MM=88. After tuning, you test ④ immediately (p. 25). *Read all the tuning and testing instructions before playing.*

Tuning ④

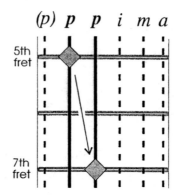

Place i, m, a on ③, ②, ①.

- *Play the 5th-fret harmonic of ⑤.*
- *Play the 7th-fret harmonic of ④.*
- *Dampen ⑥ with p.*

Step 1: Lower ④ so that beating is clearly heard.

Step 2: Raise ④ to where beating stops.

Step 3: Slightly sharpen ④ to beat at approximately MM=88.

Test ④ immediately (p. 25).

If you have trouble tuning, immediately start over from Step 1.

Approximate Beat Rates

The given beat rates for tuning each string are approximate figures. They're meant to be used as guides. The rates were determined by tuning numerous properly-set-up guitars and averaging the results. Universally accurate rates can't be provided because guitars vary somewhat in their fretting and setup. The rates for tuning your guitar may differ slightly from the given rates. At first, tune the above unison close to the given rate, then test. For ④ to be in tune, the unison must be adjusted to beat. If you tune it *beatless* and your guitar is properly set up (p. 7), ④ will play flat. See: *Why this Tuning System Works* (p. 57) for an explanation.

Testing ④

The fourth string is tested by comparing its *fretted note* at the 7th fret with the 12th-fret harmonic of ⑤. When ④ is in tune, these pitches are identical and create a beatless unison. Be sure to fret ④ gently. Avoid vibrato or pulling ④ out of tune.

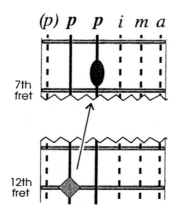

Place i, m, a on ③, ②, ①.

- *Play the 12th-fret harmonic of ⑤.*
- *Play the 7th-fret note of ④* (not harmonic).
- *Dampen ⑥ with p.*

Listen for beats as both pitches sustain.

If the test is *beatless,* ④ is in tune—you're finished tuning ④.

If you hear *beating,* ④ is out of tune—re-tune ④ (p. 24).

Exact Beat Rates

Once the above test is beatless, you can determine the exact beat rate to tune this string on your particular guitar. Simply play the tuning unison (p. 24) and listen to the beats. This is the correct rate to tune the string, assuming your guitar is properly set up. Memorize the feel of this rate by playing the tuning unison, then vocalizing and directing along with the beats. Locate this rate on your metronome and write it down.

Tuning and Testing the Third String

The third string is sharpened to the same approximate beat rate as ④. Again, carefully read all the tuning and testing instructions before playing. Be sure that both ⑤ and ④ are accurately tuned (pp. 22-25).

Tuning ③

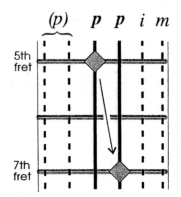

Place *i & m* on ② & ①.

- *Play the 5th-fret harmonic of ④.*
- *Play the 7th-fret harmonic of ③.*
- *Dampen ⑥ & ⑤ with p.*

Step 1: Lower ③ so that beating is clearly heard.

Step 2: Raise ③ to where beating stops.

Step 3: Slightly sharpen ③ to beat at approximately MM=88.

Test ③ immediately.

Re-play the harmonics as soon as they fade and beats become inaudible.
If ③ sustains only briefly, sound the unison before each step.
Start over from Step 1 if you have trouble.

Tuning Tips

Play clear harmonics (p. 11). Play rest stroke with *p*, near the bridge.

Swiftly grasp and turn the tuning knob. The sooner you grasp, the more time there is to tune before the harmonics fade.

Check ③'s intonation. Thick nylon 3rd strings often play sharp. Repeat the Setup Test (p. 7) if you're unsure whether ③ plays in tune. Accurate intonation often requires minor saddle adjustment.

Testing ③

The third string is tested by comparing its 2nd-fret note with the 12th-fret harmonic of ⑤. When ③ is in tune, these pitches are identical and create a beatless unison. As shown below, be sure to play ③ rest stroke with *i* for full tone and to dampen ④.

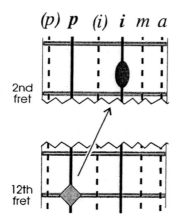

Place i, m, a on ③, ②, ①.

- *Play the 12th-fret harmonic of ⑤.*
- *Dampen ⑥ with p.*
- *Play the 2nd-fret note of ③ rest stroke with i, damping ④ with i.*

Listen for beats as both pitches sustain.

If the test is *beatless*, ③ is in tune—you're finished tuning ③.

If you hear *beating*, ③ is out of tune—re-tune ③ (p. 26).

Testing Tip

Sharp or flat? To clarify whether an out-of-tune string is sharp or flat, play the test pitches as follows:

- *Play the reference pitch on ⑤:* **listen to the pitch.**
- *Dampen all strings.*
- *Play the test pitch:* **compare the pitches.**

Tuning and Testing the Sixth String

The sixth string is *flatted* to a slower beat rate of approximately MM=66 using the two-step procedure from Exercise 5 (p. 20). First, memorize the MM=66 rate by vocalizing and directing with then without the metronome (p. 18). Next, read all the instructions before playing.

Tuning ⑥

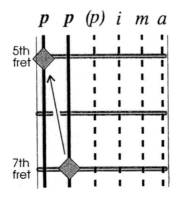

Place i, m, a on ③, ②, ①.

- *Play the 7th-fret harmonic of* ⑤.

- *Play the 5th-fret harmonic of* ⑥.
  (Play *free stroke** with *p* to avoid damping ⑤)

- *Dampen* ④ *with p.*

Step 1: Lower ⑥ so that beating is clearly heard.

Step 2: Raise ⑥ just <u>below</u> beatless to beat at approx. MM=66.

Test ⑥ immediately.

Tuning Tips

*Play ⑤ **first*** to clearly establish the reference pitch for tuning ⑥.

Prevent accidentally damping ⑤. Left hand: touch ⑥ on the *side* of the string away from ⑤. Right hand: play ⑥ *free stroke* with *p*.

Develop a feel for the beat rate. Again, the given rates are only guides. At first, tune close to the given rate, then test. Once the test is beatless, play the tuning unison and listen to the beats. This is the correct tuning beat rate, assuming your guitar is properly set up.

*****Free stroke:** play ⑥ so that *p* passes freely over and doesn't contact ⑤.

Testing ⑥

The sixth string is tested by comparing its 12th-fret harmonic with the 7th-fret note of ⑤. Be sure to fret ⑤ gently to avoid pulling it out of tune.

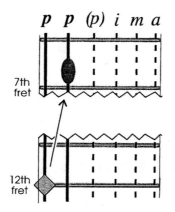

Place i, m, a on ③, ②, ①.

- *Play the 12th-fret harmonic of ⑥.*
- *Play the 7th-fret note of ⑤* (not harmonic).
- *Dampen ④ with p.*

Listen for beats as both pitches sustain.

If the test is *beatless,* ⑥ is in tune—you're finished tuning ⑥.

If you hear *beating,* ⑥ is out of tune—re-tune ⑥ (p. 28).

Tuning & Testing Tips

Always <u>raise</u> a string into tune. This removes slack from the tuning gear and helps the string *stay* in tune.

If you hear additional beating: Sometimes individual bass strings produce additional beats. If this occurs, play the *Setup Test* (p. 7) to ensure that the strings aren't defective. Replace any defective or worn string. If they're in good condition, either ignore the beating or replace the string that causes it.

Tuning and Testing the Second String

The second string is *flatted* to a slow beat rate of approximately MM=56. First, vocalize and direct this rate with then without the metronome (p. 18). Next, *practice playing and damping before you practice tuning*.

Tuning ②

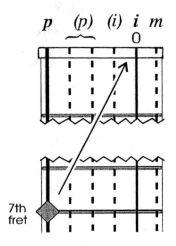

Place i & m on ② & ①.

- *Play the 7th-fret harmonic of ⑥.*

- *Dampen ⑤ & ④ with p.*

- *Play ② open, rest stroke with i, damping ③.*

Step 1: Lower ② so that beating is clearly heard.

Step 2: Raise ② just <u>below</u> beatless, to beat at approx. MM=56.

Test ② immediately.

Re-play the unison as soon as it fades and beats become inaudible. If ② sustains only briefly, sound the unison before each step. Start over from Step 1 if you have trouble.

Tuning Tips

Grasp ②'s knob promptly. Grasp the knob <u>before</u> playing ②. This enables you to tune with utmost ease and swiftness.

Turn the knob fluently. Become sensitive to the response of each string's knob.

Precisely tune the preceding strings. Be sure that ⑤, ④ & ⑥ are accurately tuned before tuning ②.

Testing ②

The second string is tested against both ④ and ⑤.

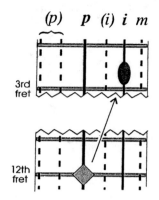

Place i & m on ② & ①.

- *Play the 12th-fret harmonic of ④.*

- *Dampen ⑥ & ⑤ with p.*

- *Play the 3rd-fret note of ②*
  rest stroke with i, damping ③.

Listen for beats as both pitches sustain.

Test ② again in relation to ⑤.

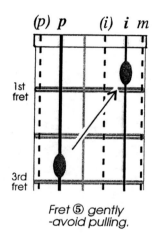

Fret ⑤ gently
-avoid pulling.

Place i & m on ② & ①.

- *Play the 3rd-fret note of ⑤.*

- *Dampen ⑥ with p.*

- *Play the 1st-fret note of ②*
  rest stroke with i, damping ③.

Listen for beats as both pitches sustain.

If both tests are *beatless,* ② is in tune.

If you hear *beating,* ② is out of tune—re-tune ②.

Testing Tip

Play both tests. If the results differ, check the tuning of ⑤ and ④.

Tuning and Testing the First String

The first string is *flatted* to a very slow beat rate of approximately MM=50. Begin by vocalizing and directing this rate with then without the metronome. Next, practice playing and damping before you practice tuning.

Tuning ①

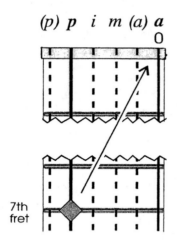

(p) p   i   m (a) a

Place i, m, a on ④, ③, ①.

- *Play the 7th-fret harmonic of* ⑤.
- *Dampen* ⑥ *with p.*
- *Play* ① *open, rest stroke with a, damping* ②.

Step 1: Lower ① so that beating is clearly heard.

Step 2: Raise ① just <u>below</u> beatless, to beat at approx. MM=50.

Test ① *immediately.*

Tuning Tips

Grasp ①*'s knob promptly,* before playing the string.

Dampen unplayed strings to maximize ease and accuracy.

Feel the beat rate. Tune ① scarcely below beatless. Listen for the beat as a wave or curve in the sound.

Testing ①

The first string is tested by comparing its 5th-fret note with the 5th-fret harmonic of ⑤.

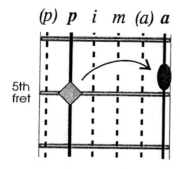

(p) p i m (a) a

5th fret

Place i, m, a on ④, ③, ①.

- *Play the 5th-fret harmonic of ⑤.*
- *Dampen ⑥ with p.*
- *Play the 5th-fret note of ①*
  rest stroke with a, damping ②.

Listen for beats as both pitches sustain.

If the test is *beatless*, ① is in tune. *Proceed to the Test Chords* (p. 34).

If you hear *beating,* ① is out of tune—re-tune ①.

Testing Tip

Sharp or flat? To clarify whether an out-of-tune string is sharp or flat, play the test pitches as follows:

- *Play the reference pitch on ⑤*: **listen to the pitch.**
- *Dampen all strings.*
- *Play the test pitch:* **compare the pitches.**

Test Chords

Testing with chords is the final step in the tuning process. After the strings are tuned individually, play the following five test chords to evaluate your tuning. Carefully read the instructions for *each chord* before playing.

- *Play each chord slowly, one string at a time.*

- *Listen for beats as each string sounds.*

- *Re-tune any string that beats significantly.*

The strings are in tune when all five test chords sound clear and harmonious with no significant beating.

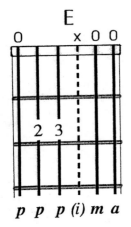

E

p p p (i) m a

- Place *p* on ⑥,
  m, a on ②, ①.

- Play ⑥, ⑤, ④, ②, ①.

- Dampen ③ with *i*.

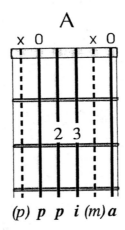

A

(p) p p i (m) a

- Place *p* on ⑤,
  i, a on ③, ①.

- Play ⑤, ④, dampen ⑥.

- Play ③, ①, dampen ②.

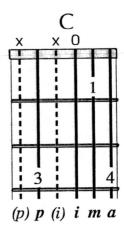

C

(p) p (i) i m a

- Place *p* on ⑤,
  i, m, a on ③, ②, ①.

- Play ⑤, dampen ⑥.

- Play ③, ②, ①,
  dampen ④ with *i*.

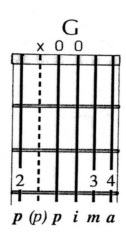

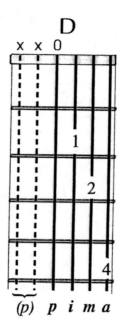

G

- Place *p* on ⑥,
  i, m, a on ③, ②, ①.
- Play ⑥, ④, dampen ⑤.
- Play ③, ②, ①.

D

- Place *p* on ④,
  i, m, a on ③, ②, ①.
- Play ④, dampen ⑥ & ⑤.
- Play ③, ②, ①.

Test Chord Tips

Fret the strings gently. Avoid vibrato or pulling any string out of tune.

Play with a clear, sustaining tone. Sound each string distinctly.

Listen! The test chords won't be perfectly beatless, they'll have very slow beat. You'll hear this beating as a slow, serene wave as each chord sustains. Listen for the chords to be *virtually* beatless. Re-tune any string that beats significantly or sounds unpleasant to your ear.*

Concise testing: Once your tuning skills are secure, aim to test as concisely as possible. Instead of playing all five test chords, two or three may suffice. Be sure to test each string at least once in a chord. Advanced guitarists may also choose to play transposed or upper-position chords.

*See: *Questions and Answers* (p. 59, paragraph 6) for additional test chord information.

Tuning Summary

After learning to tune page by page, use this summary to aid in memorizing the procedures and to reinforce good habits. Refer back to the instructions for details and tips. Read from left to right.

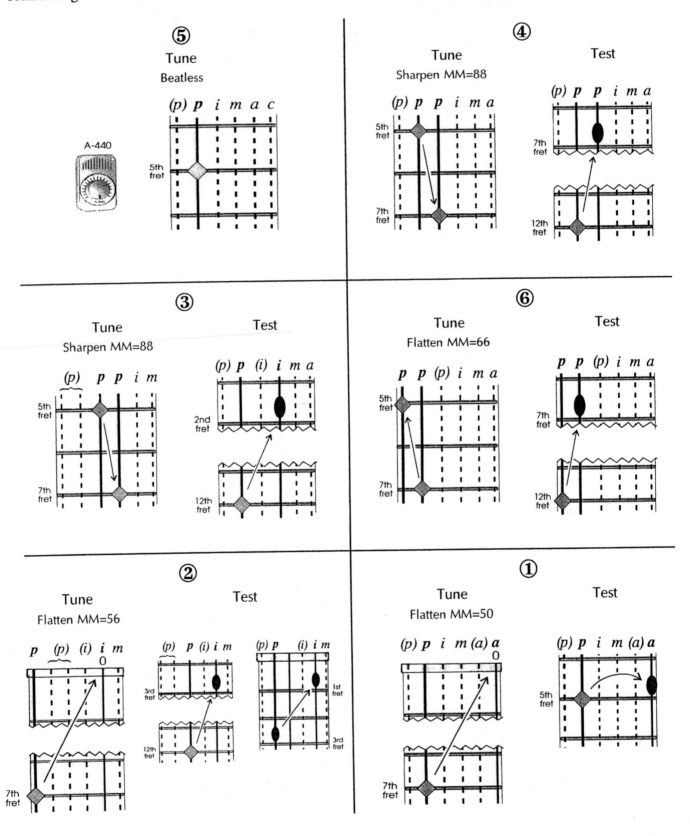

Test Chords

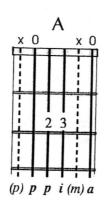

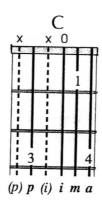

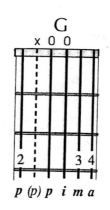

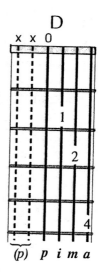

Essential Tuning Habits

Tune patiently.

Listen!

Tune first, before playing. Always begin by tuning ⑤ (p. 22).

Develop a feel for the beat rates.

Play loud, clear harmonics (p. 10).

Dampen unplayed strings.

Grasp the tuning knob immediately.

Approach from below. Always <u>raise</u> a string into tune.

Turn the tuning knobs with precision. Lower only enough to hear beats. Raise with a decisive turn.

Tune then test. Unite tuning and testing into one smooth process.

Fret the strings gently when testing.

Play clear test chords. Re-tune any string that beats significantly.

Maintain a fit guitar (pp. 5-6).

Periodically play the Setup Test to check the intonation (p. 7).

Tuning Two or More Guitars

When guitarists play together, the simplest, most accurate way to tune is by *matching open strings*. That is, each guitarist in a group tunes their open strings to those of a single reference guitar. For greatest ease and accuracy when tuning, it's essential to play loudly and dampen the unplayed strings on both the reference guitar and the guitar being tuned. For beginners, elementary string damping is appropriate (p. 39).* Experienced guitarists should eliminate all sympathetic vibrations by damping the five unplayed strings when matching each open string (pp. 40-41). Carefully read all the instructions before playing.

Matching Open Strings

1) Grasp the tuning knob of the string to be tuned.

2) Place the right-hand fingers (pp. 39-41).

- *Play the reference string.*
- *Play the same string on the out-of-tune guitar.*

Step 1: Lower the out-of-tune string so that beating is clearly heard.

Step 2: Raise the string to where beating stops—the string is now in tune.

Once all strings are tuned, experienced guitarists should play test chords (p. 34).

Tuning Tips

Tune the reference guitar first. Take time to tune precisely, *before* matching open strings.

Turn the tuning knobs fluently. Become sensitive to the response of each string's knob. Lower a string only enough to hear beats, then raise into tune with a decisive turn. Always raise, never lower into tune.

---

*For a discussion of tuning for beginning guitarists, see: *Appendix: To the Teacher* (p. 61).

Playing Open Strings
Beginning Guitarists

When matching open strings, play and dampen according to the following guidelines. It's best to tune the easiest strings first. On most guitars, the bass strings are easier to tune than the treble strings because they sustain longer. The fourth string typically is the easiest bass string to tune. Therefore, tune in the sequence: ④, ⑤, ⑥, ①, ②, ③.

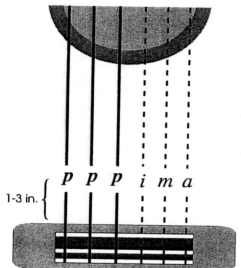

Bass Strings
Play ④ first.

- Place *i, m, a* on ③, ②, ①.

- Play forcefully with *p*,
   1-3 inches from the bridge.

   Produce a bright, loud tone.

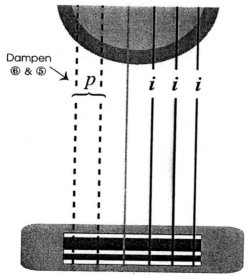

Treble Strings
Play ① first.

- Place *p* between ⑥ & ⑤.

- Play decisively rest stroke with *i*,
   next to the sound-hole.

   Produce a full, sustaining tone.

Playing Open Strings
Experienced Guitarists

Bass Strings
Play forcefully with *p,* near the bridge. Produce a bright, loud tone.

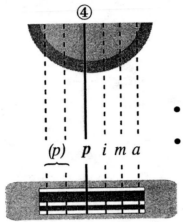

- Place *i, m, a* on ③, ②, ①.
- Play ④, dampen ⑥ & ⑤.

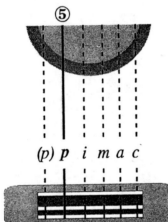

- Place *i, m, a, c,* on ④, ③, ②, ①.
- Play ⑤, dampen ⑥.

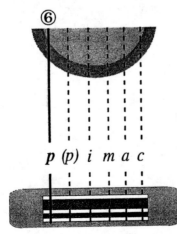

- Place *i, m, a, c,* on ④, ③, ②, ①.
- Play ⑥ rest stroke with *p,* damping ⑤.

Treble Strings
Play decisively rest stroke with *i*, next to the sound-hole.
Produce a full, sustaining tone.

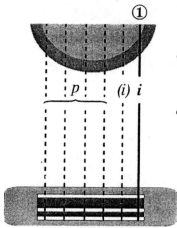

- Place *i* on ①, dampen ⑥, ⑤, ④, ③
  with the side of *p*. (Lean your hand toward *p*)
- Play ① rest stroke with *i*, damping ②.

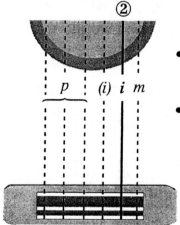

- Place *i* & *m* on ② & ①,
  dampen ⑥, ⑤, ④ with the side of *p*.
- Play ② rest stroke with *i*, damping ③.

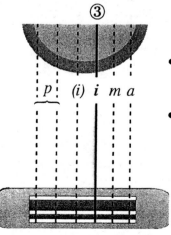

- Place *i*, *m*, *a* on ③, ②, ①,
  dampen ⑥ & ⑤ with *p*.
- Play ③ rest stroke with *i*, damping ④.

Tuning on Stage

Tuning adjustment is often needed during a performance. Secure on-stage tuning skills are essential for every performing guitarist. We need to tune quickly, confidently and in a way that doesn't detract from our artistic message. An audience doesn't notice the tuning when it's done well—they focus on the music. When tuning is done badly, a performance is seriously affected.

To tune well on stage you must first tune well in practice. Therefore, always tune with conscious precision each time you play. If you habitually tune with awareness, ease and accuracy, you'll be able to tune easily on stage. Adopt the following guidelines whenever you tune on stage. Use the pre-concert tuning tactics below to help stay in tune and minimize the need for tuning during a performance.

On-Stage Tuning Guidelines

Tune calmly and efficiently. Never rush through tuning. Concentrate on the same procedures used in practice. While tuning, don't think about the audience. Think about tuning, nothing else!

Tune no louder than necessary. Play only loud enough to hear beats.

Create silence before and after tuning. Take time to breathe and separate the tuning from the music.

Avoid tuning during applause. The audience shows their appreciation by applauding—they deserve your full attention.

Pre-Concert Tuning Tactics

Tune off stage before a performance begins. Tune precisely, well before you go on stage. Check your tuning immediately before your entrance.

Perform with your strings in top condition. Replace your strings several days before performing so they'll be stretched and stable. Avoid performing with brand-new, unstable strings. Always replace strings according to the guidelines under *Guitar Fitness* (p. 5).

Consider alternate tuning requirements. When your performances include pieces in alternate tunings, organize the program to minimize on-stage tuning changes.

Keep your guitar tuned to standard pitch (A-440). Stable string tension minimizes the need for tuning.

Alternate Tunings

Here you learn three commonly-used alternate guitar tunings: Low-D, ③=F#, and Low-G. Carefully read the instructions before playing. *Practice* by repeating the procedures many times.

Low-D Tuning

Low-D is the most frequently used alternate guitar tuning. You'll learn it in three parts. First, you tune from standard to low-D tuning (see below). Second, with ⑥=D, keeping all strings accurately tuned requires a new tuning procedure for ② because the standard one involves ⑥=E (p. 46). Finally, you tune back to standard tuning (p. 47).

Tuning from standard to low-D tuning

- **Stabilize** ⑥ (p. 43).
- **Tune** ⑥ **to D** (p. 44).
- **Play test chords** (p. 45).

Stabilizing the Sixth String
on a Classic Guitar

It's necessary to stabilize ⑥ when tuning it back and forth from E to D because a sudden tuning change will make the string unstable and cause it to go out of tune. If you suddenly *lower* ⑥ from E to D, it will go slightly sharp. If you suddenly *raise* ⑥ from D to E, it will go slightly flat. The stabilizing procedures are highly effective in keeping ⑥ more in tune.

Lowering ⑥ from E to D

Without playing:

9 half-turns

-pause briefly-

6 half-turns

Loosen ⑥**:** Turn the tuning knob 9 half-turns below E.
(A half-turn is a 180⁰ rotation of the knob)

Pause briefly—don't stretch the string.

Tighten ⑥**:** Turn the knob 6 half-turns back up toward E.

Tune ⑥ *to D* (p. 44).

These are the correct numbers of turns for the average classic guitar. For most steel-guitars, fewer turns are needed, the numbers vary. *Experiment* to find the correct numbers of turns for each steel-string guitar.

Tuning the Sixth String to D

If you're lowering ⑥ from E to D, be sure to stabilize ⑥ (p. 43) before tuning.

Tuning ⑥

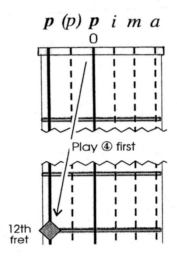

p (p) p i m a

Play ④ first

12th fret

Place i, m, a, on ③, ②, ①.

- *Play ④ open.*
- *Play the 12th-fret harmonic of ⑥.*
- *Dampen ⑤ with p.*

Step 1: Lower ⑥ so that beating is clearly heard.

Step 2: Raise ⑥ to where beating stops: ⑥ is now in tune.

(No additional test is necessary*)

Proceed to the Test Chords (p. 45).

```
┌ ─ ─ ─ ─ ─ ─ ─ ─ ─ ─ ─ ─ ─ ─ ─ ─ ─ ┐

            Tuning Tips

Play ④ first to establish the reference pitch for tuning ⑥.

Play ⑥ rest stroke with p for full tone and to dampen ⑤.

└ ─ ─ ─ ─ ─ ─ ─ ─ ─ ─ ─ ─ ─ ─ ─ ─ ─ ┘
```

*See: *Questions and Answers*, page 59, paragraph 8.

Test Chords
in Low-D Tuning

When playing test chords: 1) *Fret the strings gently.* Avoid vibrato or pulling any string out of tune. 2) Play with a clear, sustaining tone. 3) Dampen unplayed strings as shown. 4) *Listen!*

- *Play each chord slowly, one string at a time.*

- *Listen for beats as each string sounds.*

- *Re-tune any string that beats significantly*

The strings are in tune when all five test chords sound clear and harmonious with no significant beating.

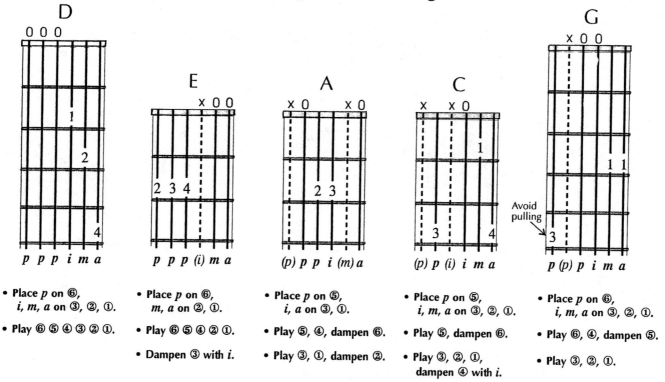

- **Place** *p* **on** ⑥,
  i, m, a **on** ③, ②, ①.

- **Play** ⑥ ⑤ ④ ③ ② ①.

- **Place** *p* **on** ⑥,
  m, a **on** ②, ①.

- **Play** ⑥ ⑤ ④ ② ①.

- **Dampen** ③ **with** *i.*

- **Place** *p* **on** ⑤,
  i, a **on** ③, ①.

- **Play** ⑤, ④, **dampen** ⑥.

- **Play** ③, ①, **dampen** ②.

- **Place** *p* **on** ⑤,
  i, m, a **on** ③, ②, ①.

- **Play** ⑤, **dampen** ⑥.

- **Play** ③, ②, ①,
  dampen ④ **with** *i.*

- **Place** *p* **on** ⑥,
  i, m, a **on** ③, ②, ①.

- **Play** ⑥, ④, **dampen** ⑤.

- **Play** ③, ②, ①.

Once your tuning skills are secure, aim to test as concisely as possible. Instead of playing all five chords, two or three may suffice. Be sure to test each string at least once in a chord.

Staying tuned in low-D tuning

If your guitar goes out of tune while in low-D tuning, tune the strings in the same order as in standard tuning. A new tuning procedure is required for ② however, because the standard one involves ⑥=E. Tune ② with the procedure below.

Tuning and Testing the Second String
in Low-D Tuning

Match the pitch of ② open to the 9th-fret note of ④.* Tuning this way is highly accurate but more difficult than listening for beats.

Tuning ②

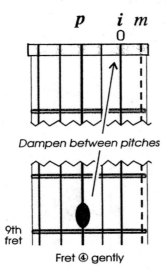

Dampen between pitches

9th fret

Fret ④ gently

Place i & m on ② & ①.

- *Play the 9th-fret note of ④.*
  Listen to the pitch.

- *Dampen all strings & grasp ②'s knob.*

- *Play ② open, rest stroke with i.*

Compare pitches, lower ② slightly, then raise ② so the pitches are identical.

Test ② immediately, using the standard procedure (p. 31)

*You can also match ② open with the 4th-fret note of ③. However, most classic guitarists find the 9th-fret note of ④ easier to match accurately.

Tuning from low-D to standard tuning

- **Stabilize ⑥** (p. 47).
- **Tune ⑥ to E** (p. 28).
- **Play test chords** (p. 34).

Stabilizing the Sixth String
on a Classic Guitar

Raising ⑥ from D to E

Without playing:

5 half-turns

-gently stretch the string-

2 half-turns

Tighten ⑥: Turn the tuning knob 5 half-turns above D.
(A half-turn is a 180^0 rotation of the knob)

Gently stretch the string with the right hand.

Loosen ⑥: Turn the knob 2 half-turns back down toward D.

Tune ⑥ to E (p. 28), then play test chords (p. 34).

The stabilizing procedures are highly effective, but not perfect. Therefore after a sudden tuning change, periodically check ⑥'s tuning until you're certain it's fully stable.

③=F# Tuning

This alternate tuning is used by classic guitarists to play Renaissance lute and vihuela music. You'll learn it in two parts. First, you tune from standard to ③=F# tuning (see below). Second, you tune back to standard tuning (p. 51). There are also important considerations when a capo is used (p. 49). All strings other than ③ are tuned with the standard procedures. Before beginning, tune accurately in standard tuning. Next, read the instructions before playing.

Tuning from standard to ③=F# tuning

- **Stabilize** ③ (p. 48).
- **Tune** ③ **to F#** (p. 49).
- **Attach a capo** (p. 49).
- **Play test chords** (p. 50).

Stabilizing the Third String
on a Classic Guitar

It's necessary to stabilize ③ when tuning it back and forth from G to F# because a sudden tuning change will make the string unstable and cause it to go out of tune. If you suddenly *lower* ③ from G to F#, it will go slightly sharp. If you suddenly *raise* ③ from F# to G, it will go slightly flat. The stabilizing procedures are highly effective in keeping ③ more in tune.

Lowering ③ from G to F#

Without playing:

7 half-turns

-pause
briefly-

Loosen ③: Turn the tuning knob 7 half-turns below G.
(A half-turn is a 180⁰ rotation of the knob)

Pause briefly—don't stretch the string.

$5\frac{1}{2}$ **half-turns**

Tighten ③: Turn the knob 5½ half-turns back up toward G.

Tune ③ *to F#* (p. 49).

The stabilizing procedures are effective, but not perfect. Therefore after a sudden tuning change, periodically check ③'s tuning until you're certain it's fully stable.

Tuning the Third String to F#

If you're lowering ③ from G to F#, be sure to stabilize ③ (p. 48) before tuning.

Tuning ③

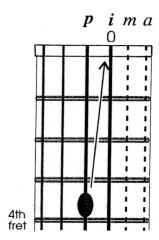

Place i, m, a on ③, ②, ①.

- *Play the 4th-fret note of ④.*
  Listen to the pitch.

- *Dampen all strings & grasp ③'s knob.*

- *Play ③ open, rest stroke with i.*

Compare pitches, lower ③ slightly, then raise ③ so the pitches are identical.

Test ③ immediately using the standard procedure (p. 27).
(Play ③ one fret higher to compensate for the new tuning)

Using a Capo

When playing in this tuning, guitarists usually use a capo on the 3rd fret to achieve a higher pitch and a more transparent, lute-like tone. Before attaching a capo, make certain all strings are accurately tuned. Next, attach the capo carefully—avoid bending the strings. After attaching the capo, check your tuning with test chords (p. 50).

When making minor tuning adjustments with a capo on, it's usually necessary to tug on the string being tuned in order to help it move under the capo. When raising a string into tune, use the left-hand 1st finger and gently push on the string behind the head nut. Remove the capo to make major tuning adjustments and before tuning ③ back to G (p. 51).

Test Chords
in ③=F# Tuning

When playing test chords: 1) *Fret the strings gently.* Avoid vibrato or pulling any string out of tune. 2) Play with a clear, sustaining tone. 3) Dampen unplayed strings as shown. 4) *Listen!*

- *Play each chord slowly, one string at a time.*

- *Listen for beats as each string sounds.*

- *Re-tune any string that beats significantly.*

The strings are in tune when all five test chords sound clear and harmonious with no significant beating.

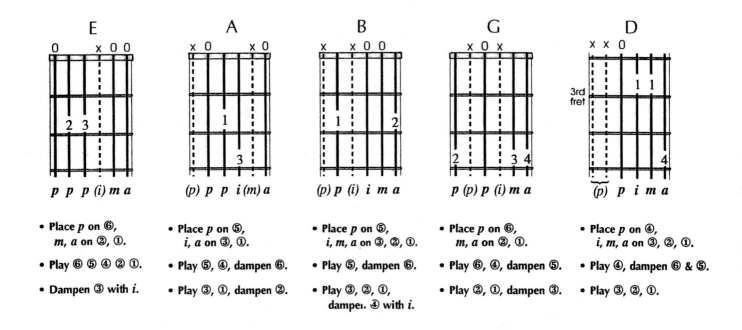

	E	A	B	G	D
	p p p (i) m a	*(p) p p i (m) a*	*(p) p (i) i m a*	*p (p) p (i) m a*	*(p) p i m a*

- **Place *p* on ⑥,** *m, a* on ②, ①.
- **Play** ⑥ ⑤ ④ ② ①.
- **Dampen** ③ with *i*.

- **Place *p* on ⑤,** *i, a* on ③, ①.
- **Play** ⑤, ④, dampen ⑥.
- **Play** ③, ①, dampen ②.

- **Place *p* on ⑤,** *i, m, a* on ③, ②, ①.
- **Play** ⑤, dampen ⑥.
- **Play** ③, ②, ①, dampen ④ with *i*.

- **Place *p* on ⑥,** *m, a* on ②, ①.
- **Play** ⑥, ④, dampen ⑤.
- **Play** ②, ①, dampen ③.

- **Place *p* on ④,** *i, m, a* on ③, ②, ①.
- **Play** ④, dampen ⑥ & ⑤.
- **Play** ③, ②, ①.

Once your tuning skills are secure, aim to test as concisely as possible. Instead of playing all five chords, two or three may suffice. Be sure to test each string at least once in a chord.

Tuning from ③=F# to standard tuning

- **Remove the capo.**
- **Stabilize ③** (p. 51).
- **Tune ③ to G** (p. 26).
- **Play test chords** (p. 34).

Stabilizing the Third String
on a Classic Guitar

Raising ③ from F# to G

Without playing:

3 half-turns

*-gently stretch
the string-*

2 half-turns

Tighten ③: Turn the tuning knob 3 half-turns above F#.
(A half-turn is a 180⁰ rotation of the knob)

Gently stretch the string with the right hand.

Loosen ③: Turn the knob 2 half-turns back down toward F#.

Tune ③ to G (p. 26), then play test chords (p. 34).

The stabilizing procedures are highly effective, but not perfect. Therefore after a sudden tuning change, periodically check ③'s tuning until you're certain it's fully stable.

Low-G Tuning

Low-G tuning, where ⑥=D and ⑤=G, is used by classic guitarists to play music by Granados, Barrios and others. You'll learn it in three parts. First, you tune from standard to low-G tuning (see below). Second, *staying* tuned in low-G involves a new overall tuning plan since ⑤ can no longer function as a reference (pp. 54-55). Finally, you tune back to standard tuning (p. 56). Carefully read the instructions before playing. Practice by repeating the procedures many times.

Tuning from standard to low-G tuning

- **Stabilize ⑥, then stabilize ⑤.** Use the same procedure for each string. Without playing, turn the tuning knob 9 half-turns down. Pause briefly. Then turn the knob 6 half-turns up (p. 43).
- **Tune ⑥ to D** (p. 44).
- **Tune ⑤ to G** (p. 52).
- **Play test chords** (p. 53).

Tuning the Fifth String to G

⑤ is tuned to G similar to the way ⑥ is tuned to D. When tuning from standard to low-G tuning, be sure to stabilize ⑥ & ⑤ (above) and tune ⑥ to D (p. 44) *before* tuning ⑤.

Tuning ⑤

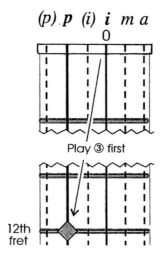

Play ③ first

12th
fret

Place i, m, a on ③, ②, ①.

- *Play ③ open, rest stroke with i, damping ④.*
- *Play the 12th-fret harmonic of ⑤.*
- *Dampen ⑥ with p.*

Step 1: Lower ⑤ to beating.

Step 2: Raise ⑤ to where beating stops.
(No additional test is necessary)

Proceed to the Test Chords (p. 53).

Test Chords
in Low-G Tuning

When playing test chords: 1) *Fret the strings gently.* Avoid vibrato or pulling any string out of tune. 2) Play with a clear, sustaining tone. 3) Dampen unplayed strings as shown. 4) *Listen!*

- *Play each chord slowly, one string at a time.*

- *Listen for beats as each string sounds.*

- *Re-tune any string that beats significantly.*

The strings are in tune when all four test chords sound clear and harmonious with no significant beating.

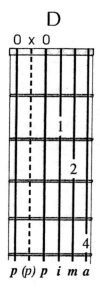

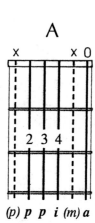
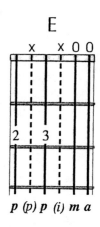

G	A	D	E
(p) p p i m a	*(p) p p i (m) a*	*p (p) p i m a*	*p (p) p (i) m a*
• Place *p* on ⑤, *i, m, a* on ③, ②, ①.	• Place *p* on ⑤, *i, a* on ③, ①.	• Place *p* on ⑥, *i, m, a* on ③, ②, ①.	• Place *p* on ⑥, *m, a* on ②, ①.
• Play ⑤, ④, dampen ⑥.	• Play ⑤, ④, dampen ⑥.	• Play ⑥, ④, dampen ⑤.	• Play ⑥, ④, dampen ⑤.
• Play ③, ②, ①.	• Play ③, ①, dampen ②.	• Play ③, ②, ①.	• Play ②, ①, dampen ③.

Once your tuning skills are secure, aim to test as concisely as possible. Instead of playing all four chords, two or three may suffice. Be sure to test each string at least once in a chord.

Staying tuned in low-G tuning

With ⑤=G, the standard tuning procedures involving ⑤ aren't effective. Because ⑤ can no longer function as a reference, staying tuned in low-G tuning requires a new overall plan. In this alternate tuning, ④ is the principal reference string with ③ serving as a secondary reference. After tuning ⑥ to D and ⑤ to G, use the procedures indicated in the box below to keep your guitar accurately tuned.

> - **Tune ④ to standard pitch** (p. 54).
> - **Tune ⑥ to D** (p. 44).
> - **Tune and test ③** (p. 55).
> - **Tune ⑤ to G** (p. 52).
> - **Tune and test ②:** use the low-D procedures (p. 46).
> - **Tune and test ①** (p. 55).
> - **Play test chords** (p. 53).

Tuning the Fourth String to Standard Pitch
in Low-G Tuning

The fourth string is tuned to the A-440 from your metronome.
You'll sharpen ④ so that the 7th-fret harmonic beats at approximately MM=88.

Tuning ④

A-440

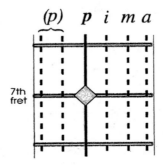

7th fret

Place i, m, a on ③, ②, ①.

- *Sound the A-440.*
- *Play the 7th-fret harmonic of ④.*
- *Dampen ⑥ & ⑤ with p.*

Step 1: Lower ④ so that beating is clearly heard.

Step 2: Raise ④ to where beating stops.

Step 3: Sharpen ④ to beat at approximately MM=88.

Next, tune ⑥ (p. 44), then tune ③ (p. 55).

Tuning and Testing the Third String
in Low-G Tuning

Tune ③ using the standard procedure (p. 26).

Testing ③

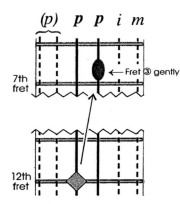

Place *i & m* on ② & ①.

- *Play the 12th-fret harmonic of ④.*
- *Play the 7th-fret note of ③.*
- *Dampen ⑤ & ⑥ with p.*

Listen for beats as both pitches sustain.

Next, tune ⑤ (p. 52), tune ② (p. 46), then tune ① (p. 55).

Tuning and Testing the First String
in Low-G Tuning

Tuning ①

- *Play the 5th-fret note of ②.*
  Listen to the pitch.

- *Dampen all strings.*

- *Play ① open.*

**Compare pitches, lower ① slightly,
then raise ① so the pitches are identical.**

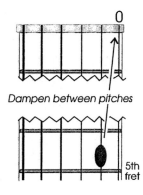

Dampen between pitches

Testing ①

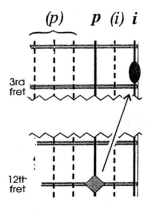

Place *i* on ①.

- *Play the 12th-fret harmonic of ③.*
- *Dampen ④, ⑤, ⑥ with the side of p.*
- *Play the 3rd-fret note of ①, rest stroke with i.*

Listen for beats as both pitches sustain.

Proceed to the Test Chords (p. 53).

Tuning from low-G to standard tuning

- **Stabilize ⑤, then stabilize ⑥.** Use the same procedure for each string. Without playing, turn the tuning knob 5 half-turns up. Gently stretch the string. Turn the knob 2 half-turns down (p. 47).
- **Tune ⑤ to A** (p. 56).
- **Tune ⑥ to E** (p. 28).
- **Play test chords** (p. 34).

Tuning the Fifth String from G to A

Using ④ as a reference, you'll flatten ⑤ to MM=88. First, stabilize both ⑤ & ⑥ (above).

Tuning ⑤

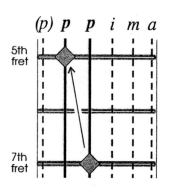

Place i, m, a on ③, ②, ①.

- *Play the 7th-fret harmonic of ④.*
- *Play the 5th-fret harmonic of ⑤.*
- *Dampen ⑥ with p.*

Step 1: Lower ⑤ to beating.

Step 2: Raise ⑤ just <u>below</u> beatless, to approximately MM=88.

Testing ⑤

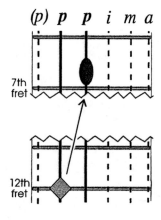

Place i, m, a on ③, ②, ①.

- *Play the 12th-fret harmonic of ⑤.*
- *Play the 7th-fret note of ④.*
- *Dampen ⑥ with p.*

Listen for beats as both pitches sustain.

Next, tune ⑥ to E (p. 28), then play test chords (p. 34).

Conclusion

Playing in tune is a cornerstone of good musicianship. If you've learned this system correctly, you should now be certain *exactly* how to tune your guitar. To continue refining your skills, always reinforce the Essential Tuning Habits (p. 37) each time you pick up your guitar to play. The enjoyment of playing in tune is the reward for patiently learning accurate tuning skills.

Why this Tuning System Works

In order to tune well, it isn't necessary to understand *why* this system works—you only must know *how* to tune. However, most guitarists are curious regarding the concepts behind this system's design. The following concise explanation addresses the main points.

Review: This system is designed around the premise that the best way to tune is by listening for beats (p. 15). To begin tuning, the fifth string is tuned to A-440 (p. 22). Next, each string is individually tuned and tested (pp. 23-33). Finally, the strings are tested with chords (pp. 34-35). Be sure you understand the difference between tuning and testing: *tuning* is the act of adjusting a string's pitch; *testing* evaluates tuning accuracy.

To listen for beats while tuning is adjusted, two pitches must be sounding as the tuning knob is turned. Since the left hand turns the knobs, no fretted pitches can be used. Therefore, tuning adjustment involves unisons comprised of pitches produced by harmonics or open strings. These sustain without left hand involvement, freeing the hand to turn the knobs. After tuning is adjusted, a string is tested with a unison involving a fretted pitch. When the tuning unisons are adjusted to the correct beat rate, then the testing unisons are beatless. To prevent compounding any errors, in standard tuning all strings are tested against the fifth string.

Background: Guitar frets are positioned and the strings are tuned so that all keys sound equally in tune. This is called *equal temperament*. In equal temperament, only octaves and unisons are tuned to sound beatless. All other intervals are tempered (i.e. altered) to varying degrees and will beat when sounded. Some intervals beat rapidly. For example, major thirds. Certain other intervals beat slowly. Again, octaves and unisons are the only beatless, *untempered* intervals in equal temperament.

Why it works: In standard tuning, the tuning unisons are adjusted to beat so that the testing unisons will be beatless. The difference between these unisons—why one beats and the other is beatless—is that the tuning unisons use 7th-fret harmonics and the testing unisons do not.

To understand the special nature of 7th-fret harmonics, first consider how harmonics are produced, then examine those at the 5th and 12th frets. A harmonic is produced without fretting a string. As a result, it isn't subject to the tempering of a fretted pitch. Therefore, harmonics produce *untempered* pitches. A harmonic at the 12th fret sounds one untempered octave above the open string. A harmonic at the 5th fret sounds two untempered octaves above the open string. Since guitars are tuned in equal temperament where octaves are untempered, the pitches produced by 5th and 12th-fret harmonics are perfectly in tune with their equivalent fretted pitches. All the testing unisons should be beatless because they compare the pitch produced by a 5th or 12th-fret harmonic with the equivalent fretted pitch. When a guitar is properly set up and tuned, these pitches are identical.

A harmonic at the 7th fret sounds an octave plus an *untempered fifth* above the open string. Since fifths are tempered in equal temperament, the untempered pitches produced by 7th-fret harmonics are not in tune with any other pitch produced on a guitar. In fact, 7th-fret harmonics are slightly sharp of their equivalent equal-tempered pitches.

In standard tuning, each tuning unison involves a 7th-fret harmonic plus either a 5th-fret harmonic or an open string. One pitch of a tuning unison is in equal temperament, the other pitch is a 7th-fret harmonic which isn't in the temperament. As a result, the pitches differ slightly and the unison beats when accurately tuned. The amount of beating is similar for all properly-set-up guitars. Therefore, approximate tuning beat rates are given in the instructions. However, exact rates are individually determined by each guitar's setup and design (see the text boxes, pp. 24-25).

Questions and Answers

Q: Why is all this instruction necessary in order to learn how to tune a guitar?

A: To develop consistently accurate tuning habits, tuning is best learned in a systematic way. Conventional tuning systems and instructions have proven ineffective for most guitarists. After teaching and observing hundreds of guitarists, I've encountered few who could tune securely using conventional methods. Few materials have been available for *learning* how to tune. I developed this booklet to provide the materials needed to learn accurate tuning skills. Guitarists tune more easily and accurately using this system than with any other I'm aware of.

Q: But isn't it difficult to hear beats and recognize beat rates?

A: Experienced guitarists sometimes have difficulty hearing beats if they're in the habit of ignoring beats. Most students have no trouble hearing them and quickly learn to recognize rates. Of the skills involved in tuning—*playing* clearly, *listening* astutely, and *adjusting* precisely—students often face more challenges playing and adjusting than they do listening. Hearing beats is easy when you play clearly and turn the knobs fluently. For example, beginning guitarists can usually match an open string with ease (p. 38) once they learn to play a string and turn a tuning knob. Recognizing subtle differences in beat rates is easier than recognizing subtle differences in pitch.

Q: Why not use the 5th-fret=open string tuning method?

A: Although it is physically simple and works perfectly in theory, in actual practice the 5th-fret method is so difficult that it seldom produces accurate results. This is mainly because:
1) errors are compounded as you tune from string to string; 2) you can't listen for beats as tuning is adjusted—instead, you must rely on the difficult skill of precise pitch discrimination.

Q: Why not tune with open strings exclusively, instead of playing unisons involving harmonics?

A: Unisons produce much clearer beating, making it far easier to tune quickly and precisely.

Q: How long does it take to learn this tuning system?

A: From a few weeks to many months may be needed to *securely* learn standard tuning. It varies with each guitarist's previous tuning experience, technical ability, aural skills and study habits. Once skilled, guitarists can typically tune in one to two minutes.

Q: What if a guitar tunes to beat rates *vastly* different from those given in the instructions? For example, if ④ tests in tune when its tuning unison is tuned beatless?

A: The guitar plays out of tune. Carefully repeat the Setup Test (p. 7). Occasionally, guitars have intonation defects which the Setup Test doesn't reveal. If you're uncertain whether your guitar plays in tune, have a technician evaluate its intonation.

Q: Is it necessary to tune the unisons to an *exact* beat rate?

A: You only must tune *close* to the correct rate. The tests reveal whether tuning is acceptable. To tune easily, you must develop a *feel* for each string's tuning beat rate.

Q: Must the testing unisons be *perfectly* beatless?

A: Virtually beatless is usually acceptable, though perfectly beatless is ideal. The test chords will reveal whether each string is acceptably tuned.

Q: Should the test chords be *perfectly* beatless?

A: No, they should sound *virtually* beatless. They have a very slow beat because they contain fifths. In equal temperament, fifths are tempered slightly flat of beatless (*equal temperament* is defined on p. 57). You'll hear this beating as a slow, serene wave as each chord sustains. Use your aesthetic judgment and listen for beats as each string sounds. Re-tune any string that beats significantly or sounds unpleasant to your ear. The chords lack thirds because equal-tempered thirds beat rapidly and would make the test chords far more difficult to evaluate.

Q: Why are both tuning *and* testing necessary?

A: To tune quickly and accurately, you must listen for something *specific* as a string's tuning is adjusted. The tuning unisons serve this purpose by allowing you to listen for beats. However, to be certain that the strings are accurately tuned, you must test with equal-tempered pitches. The test unisons and chords serve this purpose.

Q: Why isn't ⑥ tested after being tuned to D (p. 44) or ⑤ tested after being tuned to G (p. 52)?

A: Both pitches of the tuning unison are in equal temperament. Therefore, the unison is tuned beatless. The unison simultaneously functions both for tuning *and* testing. As a result, no additional test is needed other than the test chords.

Q: Can an individual string's tuning be altered to favor a particular key?

A: Not usually. If you alter a string's tuning to favor a pitch in a particular key, the string will play out of tune for other pitches. For example, if you lower ③ to favor the open-position E-major chord, ③ will sound flat on the open-position A-major chord. Since guitars are fretted in equal temperament, the strings can typically only be tuned in equal temperament. However, advanced guitarists may occasionally make subtle tuning alterations, often as compensation for setup flaws.

Q: How important is it for beginning guitarists to use electronic guitar tuners (p. 61)?

A: It's *vital* for quickly establishing good tuning habits (p. 61). Matching open strings (p. 38) develops additional aural tuning skills. For beginners, tuning by ear is nearly impossible. Counterproductive habits result when beginners struggle to tune. Teachers may experience some of a beginner's tuning challenges by holding a guitar left-handed, then trying to tune.

Additional Reading

For general information about tuning, temperament and related topics, see *The New Grove Dictionary of Music and Musicians,* ed. Stanley Sadie (London: Macmillan, 1980). Investigate the articles *Interval* (Vol. 9: pp. 277-9), *Temperaments* (18:660-74), *Physics of Music* (14:664-7), and *Sound* (17:545-63). Many additional sources of information can be found in library collections. Search the following subjects headings: *Music—Acoustics and Physics, Musical Temperament, Sound,* and *Tuning.* For information specifically about guitar tuning, search the subject heading *Guitar—Tuning.* For magazine articles, search the *Music Index* using the key words *Guitar Tuning.* Since tuning is dependent upon guitar design, you'll also find it interesting to explore the subject heading *Guitar—Construction.* You'll encounter many additional references in the bibliographies of the texts found through these searches. For even more references, consult a librarian for additional search strategies.

About the Author

I'm a classic guitarist and a member of the artist-faculty of the North Carolina School of the Arts where I maintain an active teaching and performing schedule. I previously served on the music faculties of Michigan State University, the University of Texas at San Antonio, and Lansing Community College. As a performer, I've appeared throughout the United States as solo recitalist, chamber musician and clinician. The publication of *Tuning the Guitar by Ear* culminates a thirteen-year effort to develop and refine an effective guitar tuning system and create the materials needed to teach and learn accurate tuning skills. Readers are invited to communicate with me regarding this booklet. I welcome your comments and questions. Please send correspondence via e-mail or conventional mail to: Gerald Klickstein, School of Music, North Carolina School of the Arts, P.O. Box 12189, Winston-Salem, NC 27117-2189, USA. e-mail: klickg@ncsavx.ncarts.edu

Appendix: To the Teacher

The following is a tuning approach suitable for beginning students. With the right approach and well-maintained guitars (pp. 5-7) students are able to learn precise tuning skills quickly.

Tuning for Beginning Guitarists

This booklet presents a detailed tuning system designed for guitarists of at least modest ability. It's not suitable for beginners. For beginning guitarists, the best way to tune is with an electronic guitar tuner. Electronic tuners are simple to operate and relatively inexpensive. They're effective for all types of guitars and come with adequate instructions. I strongly recommend their use because the aural and technical skills required to tune accurately by ear are far beyond most beginners' capabilities. For children especially, electronic tuners are ideal. Young children may use them for years before they're ready to learn tuning by ear. There are four main benefits to starting with an electronic tuner:

Benefits of Electronic Tuners

• *Playing in Tune.* Students begin their studies playing in tune. As a result, they learn the sound of an in-tune guitar. This leads to developing the aural skills needed to recognize the difference between being *in tune* or *out of tune.*

• *Postponing tuning by ear.* By using a tuner, beginners can focus on the immediate concerns of learning to play. They can delay tuning by ear until they're technically prepared. In this way, they avoid the frustrations and faulty tuning *habits* of beginners who struggle with tuning.

• *Developing tuning knob control.* Using a tuner, beginners learn to adjust a string's pitch precisely. They cultivate sensitive control of the tuning knobs. When they're ready to tune by ear, this vital tuning skill is already developed. Students should be taught to first lower, then *raise* a string into tune. This removes slack from the tuning mechanism and helps a string stay in tune.

• *Enjoyment.* Beginning students typically enjoy using a tuner. As a result, they easily establish the crucial habit of always tuning accurately before playing.

In my experience, using an electronic tuner at the beginning of study builds beneficial tuning habits, facilitates rapid musical progress, and prepares students for tuning by ear. To complement the use of a tuner, I also recommend that beginners learn to tune by matching their guitar's open strings to those of their teacher's guitar (see: *Tuning Two or More Guitars,* p. 38). This develops the fundamental aural skills needed for tuning by ear. *A guitar must be properly set up* (p. 7) *and in good playing condition* (pp. 5-6) *for an electronic tuner or any tuning system to be fully effective.*

Great Music at Your Fingertips